WONDER WOMAN

MONSTER MAGIC

WRITTEN BY
LOUISE SIMONSON

ILLUSTRATED BY
DAN SCHOENING

WONDER WOMAN
CREATED BY
WILLIAM MOULTON MARSTON

STONE ARCH BOOKS
a capstone imprint

Published by Stone Arch Books in 2010
A Capstone Imprint
151 Good Counsel Drive, P.O. Box 669
Mankato, Minnesota 56002
www.capstonepub.com

Library of Congress Cataloging-in-Publication Data

Simonson, Louise.
    Monster magic / by Louise Simonson ; illustrated by Dan Schoening.
        p. cm. -- (DC super heroes. Wonder Woman)
    ISBN 978-1-4342-1884-1 (library binding) -- ISBN 978-1-4342-2260-2
(pbk.)
    [1. Superheroes--Fiction. 2. Monsters--Fiction.] I. Schoening, Dan, ill. II.
Title.
    PZ7.S605795Mo 2010
    [Fic]--dc22   2009029097

Summary: On a remote island, scientists discover an exotic plant which
they hope will lead to a medical breakthrough. Instead, when they return
to Washington, D.C., the rare fauna brings on a monstrous breakout. The
sinister sorceress, Circe, attacks the city with her magical malice. Even
Wonder Woman, the Princess of the Amazons, can't escape her cruel
charms, and if the Lasso of the Truth won't set her free, the capital city
will soon become Circe's domain.

Art Director: Bob Lentz
Designer: Emily Harris
Production Specialist: Michelle Biedscheid

Printed in the United States of America in Stevens Point, Wisconsin.
092009
005619WZS10

TABLE OF CONTENTS

CHAPTER 1

CREATURE CHAOS. 4

CHAPTER 2

MONSTER MAGIC 13

CHAPTER 3

CIRCE'S TALE. 21

CHAPTER 4

MAGICAL ATTACK 31

CHAPTER 5

VICTORY AT LAST. 40

CREATURE CHAOS

Princess Diana was visiting New York from her new home in Washington, D.C. She glanced up at the skyscrapers as she crossed Fifth Avenue. Mostly, she watched the people — men and women, young and old, workers and tourists. They were from every continent on Earth.

New York is so different from my home on Themyscira, she thought. *The noise. The bustle. The variety. The excitement. I love it!*

As she stepped onto the sidewalk, she glanced in a shiny shop window.

The glass showed the reflection of a tall young woman in a plain blue suit. Her dark hair was pulled into a bun. Diana almost didn't recognize her own reflection.

I look so modern, she thought. *I'm different in America. But then, I'd be different almost anywhere.*

Suddenly, she heard brakes screech, then a loud **CRUNCH!** as a car crashed. Horns blared and people screamed.

Diana glanced up the street. Her mouth opened in amazement. Then she began to spin, twirling so quickly that the air blurred around her. **WHOOOOSH!**

When she stopped, her dark, wavy hair was tumbling down her back. She was wearing an outfit of red, blue, and gold. She had changed into Wonder Woman!

A golden tiara sat on her head like a crown. Thick metal bracelets adorned her wrists. A Golden Lasso hung from her belt.

Wonder Woman soared into the air.

Two large monsters were charging down the middle of Fifth Avenue. They had scared drivers and caused the crash.

As she watched, a Minotaur — a giant man with the head of a bull — gored a taxi with its huge horns. A Hydra — a giant snake with nine heads — slithered and hissed as people left their cars and ran.

Wonder Woman recognized the monsters because she had grown up on the mysterious island of Themyscira, surrounded by immortal women called Amazons. Many strange and monstrous animals lived there, too.

Diana was the Amazon queen's daughter. While she was a baby, the Greek gods had given her extraordinary abilities. When she grew older, she left Themyscira for what the Amazons called Man's World. Diana wanted to use her special powers to help the people of Earth. When she arrived in the United States, the newspapers were so impressed with her deeds, they began to call her Wonder Woman.

As she flew toward the monsters, Diana wondered what they were doing in New York — and what she should do about them.

One of my gifts is a special bond with animals, she thought. *I'll try that first.*

Wonder Woman landed in front of the creatures and spoke to them gently, trying to calm them. For a moment it worked.

The Minotaur stopped its rampage. Most of the hydra's heads swayed like they were mesmerized.

Then, suddenly, two of the snake heads struck like lightning.

Just as quickly, Wonder Woman raised her arms. She blocked the poisonous blows with her thick, magical bracelets. **TWANNNGG!**

The hydra's fangs struck hard metal and it drew back in pain. Hissing and spitting, the angry monster loomed above her. Then three more of its heads struck at the same time. Once again, Wonder Woman blocked the blows with her bracelets. **CLANK!**

This isn't working, she thought. *But I have other powers I can use to stop it.*

Moving at super-speed, Wonder Woman punched the hydra on each of its chins.

In seconds, the monster snake lay on the ground with all of its heads unconscious.

SMASH! Behind her, more cars crashed. More people screamed. More horns blared. Sirens began to wail.

What now? Wonder Woman thought. She leaped into the air and looked around.

While she had been fighting the hydra, the Minotaur had charged down the street. It was flipping vehicles over as it ran. Several taxis lay on their sides. People were trapped in overturned cars. Fifth Avenue was a mess!

Wonder Woman landed and placed the cars back on their wheels. She pulled a hurt man from a wrecked taxi and lifted him into the air. Then she carried him to the ambulance that had just arrived.

When she looked around, the Minotaur had disappeared.

It can't just be gone, Wonder Woman thought. *Maybe I need to search from above.*

She leaped into the air, looking up and down the street. Then she heard the wail of fire engines from somewhere nearby.

Now what's happening? she thought.

As she flew toward the fire, the blare of sirens grew louder. The air grew so thick with smoke that she could hardly see the buildings beside her or the street below.

Suddenly, she heard a roar that was louder than the screaming sirens. A huge fireball appeared in the smoke. It was coming right at her!

THWOOOOMMM!!

CHAPTER 2

MONSTER MAGIC

Wonder Woman zipped aside. The fireball roared past her. **POOF!** It struck the balcony of a tall apartment building.

Hisssssss The awning that shaded the balcony burst into flames. Then it crumbled into ash.

Out of the smoke came a giant reptile covered with blood-red scales. It flew toward Wonder Woman with huge flapping wings. Its mouth opened wide. As it started to roar, she could see a bright blaze growing in its throat.

A dragon! she thought.

Then another fireball burst from its huge mouth. **WHOOOOSH!**

Wonder Woman dodged to one side quickly. She was super-strong, but she wasn't invulnerable. If the dragon's fire touched her, it would burn her.

The dragon will hurt anyone who gets in its way, Wonder Woman thought. *I have to find a way to stop it!*

As she watched, the dragon flew past Wonder Woman, heading for a tall skyscraper covered with mirrored glass windows. A sign on top of the building read Marston Research Laboratories.

As the dragon neared the building, it opened its mouth and growled.

The dragon, reflected in the mirrored windows, looked like it was roaring back.

THWOOOOMMMMM! A fireball spewed from the dragon's mouth and hit its reflection, melting a huge hole in the glass.

It probably thinks it's fighting another dragon, Wonder Woman thought. *If I don't do something, it will crash through the windows — and the building!*

I'll need all of my powers to stop it, she thought. *But most of all, I'll need my Golden Lasso!*

She pulled the gleaming lasso from the loop on her belt. It was a gift from the goddess Hestia and was one of Wonder Woman's most prized possessions. It was made of a chain that had been magically created from tiny links of gold.

Best of all, nothing could destroy it —
not even a dragon's fire.

Wonder Woman soared after the dragon.
She whirled the Golden Lasso above her
head. Then, when she was close enough,
she threw it toward the beast.

SNAP! The loop settled over the
dragon's huge head. Wonder Woman
pulled it tight. She flew lower, planning to
leap onto the dragon's back. She hoped she
could use the lasso like a rein, and steer the
monster away from the city.

To her surprise, the dragon began to
shrink. Then its reptile body began to
transform. It lost its scales. Its wings faded
and disappeared. Then it fell.

Wonder Woman blinked in surprise.

The dragon had become a man!

The man was very frightened. He was wearing a red jogging suit, and he dangled by his waist from the loop of her Golden Lasso.

She knew that her lasso had the power to expose the truth. Anything caught in its loop would reveal its real form. It hadn't occurred to her that the dragon would turn out to be a man who had been transformed into a monster.

"What am I doing here?" the frightened man whimpered. "What's going on?"

"I'll have you on the ground in a minute," Wonder Woman called down to him. "Then maybe we can find out."

She lowered him gently to the sidewalk. Nearby, firemen were spraying water from big hoses on the burning buildings.

Wonder Woman landed beside the man.

"What happened to you?" she asked.

"I remember jogging on the path beside the river," he said. "There was a beautiful woman standing right in front of me. There was a flash of purple light. The next thing I knew, I was dangling from the end of your rope."

He didn't remember his time as a dragon. He didn't remember starting all the fires. He didn't even know who had turned him into a fire-breathing monster.

"My throat burns," he said in a raspy voice. "I don't feel so good."

Wonder Woman was helping the man out of the Golden Lasso when his mouth opened wide.

Then he screamed.

CHAPTER 3

CIRCE'S TALE

Wonder Woman whirled. Slithering toward her was another fire-breathing monster. This one had two heads — the head of a goat and the head of a lion. The front half of its body was like a lion. But its rear was a giant serpent tail.

"A chimera . . ." she muttered. "What next?"

Fireballs shot from the chimera's two mouths. **WHAM!** Double blasts of flame struck the door of the tall skyscraper. The glass shattered and melted. **KA-BOOM!**

As the chimera charged toward her, Wonder Woman made the loop of her Golden Lasso very wide. She wanted to trap both heads at once. She whirled it above her head. Then she threw it into the air.

The lasso settled over the chimera's heads. Then Wonder Woman pulled it tight.

Slowly, the two heads faded into one. The lion's paws and body became a man's arms and torso. The serpent tail split and became two legs.

Where the chimera once stood, a man in a gray suit sat on the sidewalk. "Where am I?" he asked. "What am I doing here?"

This man, too, said he had seen a beautiful woman and a flash of light. That was the last thing he remembered, until he woke up on the sidewalk.

Wonder Woman frowned. It sounded like a beautiful woman was turning people into monsters. Who could be doing it? And why?

"I'll bet the hydra I fought was really a person," Wonder Woman said to herself. "And the Minotaur, too. I need to find them and remove the enchantments before they hurt someone."

She gathered up her Golden Lasso and hooked it onto her belt, but before she could fly into the air, something huge and dark swooped down from the sky. It snatched her up in huge claws and carried her high above the city. **WHOOOOSH!**

Wonder Woman looked down at the buildings and crowded streets. Then she looked up at the monster that had grabbed her. Its front half looked like a giant eagle.

The back half of the creature looked like a giant lion. She was being carried off by a creature called a gryphon!

"At least you don't breathe fire," she said to the monster.

Wonder Woman knew she could easily break free from the monster by using her Golden Lasso to turn it back into a man. But she was curious. She wanted to see where the gryphon would take her. She hoped it would carry her to the woman who was turning men into monsters.

The gryphon was gliding toward a towering skyscraper. Wonder Woman saw a beautiful woman with lavender hair, dressed in green robes. She was standing on the rooftop garden of a penthouse apartment, looking up calmly, watching them descend.

Dipping low, the gryphon opened its claws. Wonder Woman dropped through the air and landed on the flat roof. She was now facing the lavender-haired woman.

As Wonder Woman stared at her, she saw tiny wrinkles beginning to form around the woman's eyes and mouth. She was beautiful, but she was aging quickly.

"Who are you?" Wonder Woman asked.

"My name is Circe," the woman said. "I am an enchantress."

"I figured that much out," Wonder Woman said. "What I don't know is why you've been turning people into monsters."

Circe raised her perfect eyebrows. "So they can take back what others have stolen from me," she said.

Wonder Woman frowned.

"What do you mean?" she asked.

"Unlike your people, the Amazons, I am not immortal," Circe said. "I have kept myself young for centuries by drinking a magical drink called *vitae*. I make it from a mixture of rare plants and herbs that grow on Aeaea Island where I live." As Circe spoke, several silver streaks appeared in her lavender hair.

Wonder Woman frowned. "I don't think your vitae is working," she said.

"That's because, when I returned home from a trip, I discovered that my plants were gone. I couldn't make more of my special drink," Circe said. "My crystal ball showed me what had happened. While I was away, thieves came to my island. They dug up my plants and carried them to New York. I've come to take them back!"

"And then you transformed people into monsters," Wonder Woman said. "Why?"

Circe shrugged. "Once the men were transformed, they became my servants," she said. "I sent them to get my plants back." She pointed to the Marston Research Laboratories building. "That's where the thieves took the plants."

Circe knew Wonder Woman was one of the Amazons, a race of immortal female warriors. Circe thought Wonder Woman would agree.

Instead, Wonder Woman was furious. "I saw the dragon and chimera melt the glass in that building. I should have realized that building was their target!" Wonder Woman said.

Circe sneered at her.

"Instead, you just kept lassoing my servants and turning them back into people," Circe said. "I thought you, of all people, would understand."

Wonder Woman folded her arms. "I understand why you're angry," she said. "But it's wrong to turn people into monsters and put innocent humans in danger. Remove your spells at once! Restore the men to their true forms! Do it now!"

HAHAHAHA! Circe laughed maniacally. "Oh, don't worry — my spell will wear off in a month or two. In the meantime, since you won't help me, you can join them!"

She hurled a sparkling bolt of magic straight at Wonder Woman's heart.

CHAPTER 4

MAGICAL ATTACK

Wonder Woman leaped into the air. Circe's spell swirled past her toes. The shimmering magic struck a flowering tree growing in a big clay pot. POP!

The tree began to writhe and twist. A pigeon that was sitting on a branch flew into the air, squawking in alarm.

Suddenly, the tree became a giant flower that looked like a meat-eating Venus flytrap. Its blossom reminded Wonder Woman of a purple claw. She watched in horror as its petals opened wide.

The plant snapped at Wonder Woman with its newly-formed jaws, but she quickly flew out of its way.

Wonder Woman was glad she had avoided that spell. *What would it have done to me?* she wondered. She had to make Circe remove her enchantments before someone was seriously hurt.

Wonder Woman hovered in the air, whirling her Golden Lasso above her head.

"You dodged my spell very quickly," Circe said. "But that little rope will not stop me. How would you like that spinning lasso to become a snake?"

Circe pointed. **BZZT!** A spiral of green magic shot from her finger and surrounded the whirling lasso. The magic sparkled.

Then the magic disappeared.

"Your magic can't harm my Golden Lasso," Wonder Woman said as she spun the loop faster and faster. "It reveals the truth in anyone or anything it encircles. It is a gift made by the gods, and it cannot be transformed!"

Then, quick as lightning, Wonder Woman hurled the loop at Circe. SNAP!

Circe couldn't use her magic to change the lasso, but she could use a spell to protect herself. She waved her arm and created a glittering lavender shield.

Wonder Woman's lasso struck the magic shield and bounced off. ZING!

Circe called up to the winged gryphon that was still circling overhead. "Come to me, my servant!" she shrieked.

Obediently, the monster dropped onto the roof beside Circe. The sorceress leaped onto its back.

"I've heard the stories about you, Wonder Woman, and now I see they're true!" Circe shouted as she hurled another ball of shimmering magic. "I will change you into a monster so powerful that no one will be able to stop you. You will become my most fabulous servant. You will bring me back my stolen plants!"

Wonder Woman dodged the magic burst. **FZZT!** It hit a wall and disappeared harmlessly. But a second blast hit a tiny dog, far below. The air shimmered around it, and the dog grew into a winged creature!

"Take flight, my beauty!" Circe cried. The gryphon pumped its magnificent white wings. It rose high into the air.

It seems that Circe's magic only changes living things, Wonder Woman thought, as she took off, racing above the city. *But that's bad enough. New York is full of people, animals, and plants. If she stays here, who knows how much damage she'll cause!*

Circe gave a loud laugh as she flew after Wonder Woman. "Come, my beauties!" she shouted to her monsters. "Capture our prize. Hold her steady so I can transform her. Then she will be one of you!"

Soon, other flying monsters were darting toward Wonder Woman.

Wonder Woman saw three harpies — giant vultures with the heads of women. Behind them flew the giant monster that used to be a dog, growling fiercely.

As she flew across the city, Wonder Woman dodged the harpies' claws and the snapping jaws of the monstrous dog. She zigged and zagged to avoid Circe's spells.

She knew she could stop the monsters by knocking them unconscious, or by capturing them in her Golden Lasso. She also knew that these monsters were really people. She didn't want to hurt them.

Maybe I can make Circe think I'm in trouble, Wonder Woman thought. *Then I can get them all out of the city!*

Wonder Woman dropped low, toward the street. She flew right above the cars. She slowed down a little, trying to look like she was getting tired.

Circe laughed gleefully as she hurled another magic bolt. **BZZZT!**

She was gaining on Wonder Woman — and she was having fun.

"My spells make people become the monsters they were meant to be!" Circe shouted. "It will be fun to see what kind of creature you become!"

38

CHAPTER 5

VICTORY AT LAST

In the reflection of a car window, Wonder Woman saw Circe's spell coming at her. She dodged aside quickly. The spell flew past Wonder Woman's shoulder, hit the car's shiny windshield, and bounced off.

The magic struck a tree growing near the sidewalk. There was a shimmer of magic. Then the tree pulled itself out of the pavement and walked along on its roots! It lashed its limbs around like whips.

At least it wasn't another person, Wonder Woman thought.

Then she smiled. She had just come up with a great idea!

Wonder Woman soared high into the air and looked around. She spotted the Marston Research Laboratory building. That was where Circe said the men had taken her stolen plants.

She looked behind her to make sure Circe was following. Then she flew straight toward the building made of mirrored glass.

In seconds, she could see herself reflected in the building's windows. She could see Circe, flying on the gryphon's back, right behind her.

Circe had her hand outstretched. She was getting ready to hurl another magic spell at Wonder Woman.

"I see where you're going," Circe shouted. "Even if you get my plants back, it won't save you! I'll still turn you into my monstrous servant!"

BZZT! Circe hurled the sparkling purple spell. Wonder Woman dodged to one side. The spell struck a mirrored window and bounced back — right at Circe.

It struck Circe with a blinding **FLASH!** Magical light flickered around her. Then the sorceress began to change. Her slender body widened. Her cheeks grew round. Her regal nose became flat. Little hooves appeared on the end of her stubby arms. Then she sprouted wings and a little curly tail. Circe's own spell had turned the sorceress into a flying pig!

The instant that Circe transformed, the spells she had cast were broken.

The gryphon had become a man. He could no longer fly, and was screaming as he fell toward the ground. Wonder Woman grabbed him with one hand.

With the other hand, she whirled her lasso. She captured the three women who had been harpies before they hit the ground. She landed carrying all those people. Then she caught the tiny dog, which had been a monster, in her arms.

Wonder Woman heaved a sigh. Circe's magic spells had been broken at last.

The squealing, flying pig rammed into Wonder Woman from behind. **THUD!** It sent her sprawling onto the sidewalk. Wonder Woman looked up at the pig.

"Just for that, I'm not going to use my Golden Lasso to release you!" she said.

Wonder Woman grabbed the squealing animal. "You're going to remain a pig until your spell wears off in a couple of months. It's just what you deserve!"

Wonder Woman held the squealing pig under her arm as she flew around the side of the Marston building. She found the hole the dragon had melted in the glass.

Carrying the pig, she flew inside.

A group of confused scientists in white lab coats stared at her. The head scientist stepped forward. "Wonder Woman," he said. "How can we help you?"

"Are you the men who took plants from Aeaea Island?" Wonder Woman asked.

The scientist explained that his group had been traveling the world, gathering native plants.

They had hoped that testing the plants would lead to the discovery of medicines. The scientists heard legends about Aeaea Island, so they decided to look there.

All they found were old ruins. They hadn't realized Circe was real or that she lived there. But they did take several new kinds of plants back with them.

"The ruins were probably a magical illusion that hid Circe's palace," Wonder Woman said. "Circe came here to get her plants back." She told them that Circe was now a winged pig.

The scientists looked worried. "The plants were destroyed during our study," one said.

Circe squealed angrily and tried to wiggle free. The scientists stepped back.

"Our studies showed there's nothing unusual about those plants," the scientist continued. "Maybe Circe's magic was what made them special. The plants are gone, but we did save the seeds. Will they do?"

He gave Wonder Woman an envelope filled with seeds. He told her that the seeds would soon grow if planted near water.

*   *   *

Carrying the angry, winged pig, Wonder Woman flew over the ocean, back to Aeaea Island. She soared over the ruins that concealed Circe's palace.

Wonder Woman landed beside a flowing stream. She placed the angry pig on the ground. Then Wonder Woman opened the envelope and scattered the seeds on the rich, wet soil.

"Until your spell wears off, it will be your punishment to live here as an animal, experiencing the fate you were so eager to give others," she said. "By the time you're back to normal, your plants will have grown, and you can make your magic drink. The scientists who took those plants didn't know they were your property. Leave them alone, or you will answer to me."

Circe gave a grumpy "Oink!" Then she flopped down in the mud beside the stream to watch her plants grow.

INVISIBLE PLANE
SECRET FILES

FILE NO. 3925 >>> CIRCE

ENEMY » ALLY FRIEND

OCCUPATION: ENCHANTRESS

HEIGHT: 5 ft 11 in **WEIGHT:** 145 lbs

EYES: Blue **HAIR:** Lavender

POWERS/ABILITIES: Immortality, stunning physical beauty, and magical powers that allow her to perform a variety of tricks and spells

BIOGRAPHY

Circe is a centuries-old sorceress who spends the majority of her time on the island of Aeaea. It is there where a special plant grows that Circe uses to make an elixir called vitae. It is this elixir that allows her to remain eternally youthful and beautiful. Circe also has a wide variety of magical abilities that make her an extremely dangerous foe. She can control minds, fire powerful energy blasts, create illusions, and even revive the dead! Circe loves nothing more than humiliating others, and she also loves turning human beings into animals, so extreme caution should be taken when approaching her.

POWERS

A MAGICAL MENACE!

• MIND CONTROL: Circe can control her enemies' minds, making them do whatever she wishes.

• ENERGY BLASTS: She can send volleys of destructive magical energy at her opponents.

• ILLUSION: Circe can create illusions at will in order to trick and confuse her opponents.

• TELEPORTATION: She can immediately transport herself from place to place.

• TRANSFORMATION: Circe's preferred attack method is to change people into mythical creatures.

• NECROMANCY: Since her husband, Ares, rules the underworld, Circe has some level of control over the dead, allowing her to bring them back to life.

WEAPONS

MIGHTIER THAN MAGIC . . .

Wonder Woman's magical bracelets are the perfect defense against Circe's magical attacks. Her silver armlets allow Wonder Woman to deflect or block magic, preventing damage or transformation. The Lasso of Truth is also a potent defense against Circe's magic. When Wonder Woman lassoes anyone under Circe's spells, it dispels the magic, returning the person back to normal. The unbreakable golden rope cannot be harmed by magic, making it the preferred weapon against Circe and her magical minions.

BIOGRAPHIES

Louise Simonson writes about monsters, science fiction and fantasy characters, and super heroes. She wrote the award-winning Power Pack series, several best-selling X-Men titles, *Web of Spider-man* for Marvel Comics, and *Superman: Man of Steel* and *Steel* for DC Comics. She has also written many books for kids. She is married to comic artist and writer Walter Simonson. They live in the suburbs of New York City.

Dan Schoening was born in Victoria, B.C., Canada. From an early age, Dan has had a passion for animation and comic books. Currently, Dan does freelance work in the animation and game industry and spends a lot of time with his lovely little daughter, Paige.

GLOSSARY

adorned (uh-DORND)—decorated

concealed (kuhn-SEELD)—hid something

enchantment (en-CHANT-ment)—a magic spell

illusion (i-LOO-zhuhn)—something that appears to exist but actually does not

legend (LEJ-uhnd)—a story handed down from earlier times. Legends are often based on fact, but are not completely true.

limbs (LIMZ)—parts of a body used in moving or grasping. Arms, legs, wings, and flippers are different kinds of limbs.

magnificent (mag-NIF-i-sent)—very impressive or beautiful

mesmerized (MEZ-muh-rized)—hypnotized or spellbound

regal (REE-guhl)—fit for a king or queen, or royal in nature

transformed (transs-FORMD)—made something change

DISCUSSION QUESTIONS

1. Was Circe right to be angry at the scientists who took her plants? Why or why not?

2. Wonder Woman always saves innocent people before catching criminals. What's more important — jailing the guilty, or keeping the innocent safe from harm?

WRITING PROMPTS

1. If you were struck by Circe's magical powers, what kind of crazy creature would you turn into? Describe your monstrous transformation. Then, draw a picture of your new form.

2. What will Circe do when she turns back into her normal form? Will she seek revenge? Write another chapter to this book.

3. If you could have any ability or tool that Circe or Wonder Woman uses in this book, which would you choose? What would you use it for? Write about it!

MORE NEW

WONDER WOMAN

ADVENTURES!

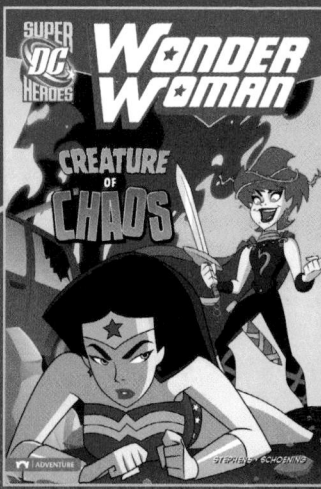

CREATURE OF CHAOS

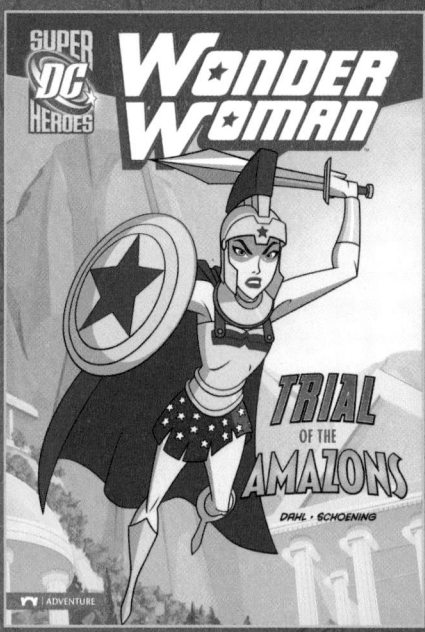

TRIAL OF THE AMAZONS

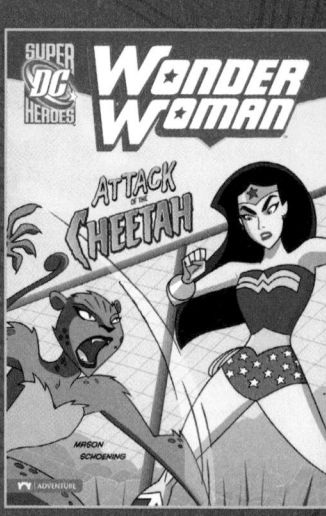

ATTACK OF THE CHEETAH